# Glamorgan
## Folk Tales
*for children*

# Glamorgan
## Folk Tales
### *for children*

CATH LITTLE

Illustrated by Peter Stevenson

*For the children of
Kitchener Primary School*

First published 2017

The History Press
The Mill, Brimscombe Port
Stroud, Gloucestershire, GL5 2QG
www.thehistorypress.co.uk

Text © Cath Little, 2017
Illustrations © Peter Stevenson, 2017

British Library Cataloguing in Publication Data.
A catalogue record for this book is available from the British Library.

ISBN 978 0 7509 7040 2

Typesetting and origination by The History Press
Printed in Great Britain by TJ International Ltd, Padstow, Cornwall

# Contents

# Acknowledgements

Thanks to my father who first told me stories, thanks to my mother, who read them to me. Thanks to my partner Luc and to my wonderful children, Rosa and Joseph, for their love and support. Thanks to all my family and especially to my Aunty Jo, who always said that I'd write a book.

With heartfelt thanks to all the children, parents and teachers at Kitchener Primary School. Thanks to Angela Harris and everyone at Family Story Club for all your listening and all your stories. Thanks to Siân Jones and Dee Kaur for your encouragement.

Thanks so much to Peter Stevenson for his delightful illustrations.

Thanks to all my storytelling friends, especially Fiona Collins, Guto Dafis, Sean Taylor, Elinor Kapp and Richard Berry who kept me company on the way and gave practical advice.

Thanks to all the people who told the stories and listened to the stories through the years and kept them alive. Thanks to the collectors who wrote them down: to Gerald of Wales, The Boys of Lewis School, Pengam and their teacher Mr T. Matthews, Alan Roderick, Ken Radford, Anthony Rees and Marie Trevelyan. Especially to Marie Trevelyan. Most of the stories in this book come from Marie Trevelyan's collection, *Folk-Lore and Folk-Stories of Wales*. We are all so lucky that she wrote the stories down.

# About the Author

Cath Little is a storyteller from Cardiff. She tells stories in schools, libraries and museums, castles, cafes and fields. She loves telling stories and she loves listening to stories. This is her first book.

# About the Illustrator

Peter is a book illustrator, storyteller, writer and folklorist, inspired by the art of visual storytelling. He lives in Aberystwyth, where he runs a storytelling festival and club, and wanders the old Welsh tramping roads, listening to the birds and anyone happy to tell him a tale and share a cake.

# Introduction

All the stories in this book are old stories that were told long ago in Glamorgan. These stories are not my stories. These stories belong to everyone. They are meant to be told.

All I have done is research and find the old stories and then write them down in a new way. I have had a lot of help from some really good listeners and readers. Here are some of the things they told me:

'These stories are enchanting, mysterious and excellent.' – Jessica

'I really liked the stories. It was interesting to find out about the places and hear the names of people who lived long ago.' – Oliver

'My favourite story was the one about the box. I really wanted to know what was in that box.' – Asiya

'I think "The Lady of Ogmore Down" teaches us to never give up and always try your best no matter what.' – Prubjort

'These stories have mystery and give us pictures in our imaginations.' – Emily and Ayesha

'I was really surprised when the snakes were friends and healed the girl.' – Meju

'I like the sad stories best.' – Bhapur

'I like the one where the old man asks the young man to go under the magic hazel tree. My heart was beating fast when I thought the warriors were going to wake up. You made the story even better by adding Welsh words.' – Ahammed

'I liked the part where the animals and the trees and the people all helped each other.' – Anisha

These stories are presents. They are presents from the people who lived here long ago. A story is the best present. You can give it away and you can keep it for yourself. We can keep these ancient stories and pass them on to people in the future. And maybe these old stories will inspire us to make up some new stories. And we could pass those on too!

# 1

# The White Lady in the Woods

There was a White Lady in the woods near the school I went to when I was a child. I went to PenyrHeol School, the school at the top of the road. There were woods next to the school with a stream running through. That's where the White Lady lived. She wandered all alone through the trees and washed her hands in the stream. All the children knew she was there, though the teachers never mentioned her. I felt sorry for her. She had no one to play with, only the grass snakes and the green frogs and the little fish in the water. I was a bit scared of her too. I wanted to see her, but I didn't want to see her. There was a dark, damp shadowy place under the school buildings. Some children said they had seen the White Lady there. They said her dress was torn and tattered like spiders' webs. 'I dare you to go down there!'

When I grew up and became a storyteller, I found that there are lots of stories about *Ladi Wen*, the White Lady. I have put one of them in this book, 'The Three White Roses'. I also found out that my old school was named after the farm that used to be there, Pen yr Heol Farm. One of my teachers at school was called Mr Richardson. Mr Richardson was an inspiring teacher who loved history and made me love history too. He told us that a thousand years ago there was a Celtic tribe living on the land where our school was built. The Celtic tribe was called the Silures. The Silures lived in roundhouses made of mud and straw. And they loved stories.

White Lady

I wonder how long the White Lady has been there. Maybe the children who lived in Pen yr Heol Farm told stories about the White Lady. And maybe the Silure children told stories about the White Lady. Maybe they did. Maybe she's been there all the time.

# 2

# The Salmon Children

Once there was a sister and a brother who grew up in a forest. Their names were Meidwen and Ieuan and they grew up in Coed Duon, the Blackwood. They climbed to the tops of the trees. They swam in the River Rhymney. All the birds and the animals were their friends. Small birds would sit on their shoulders and sing to them. Shy deer and rabbits would come to their open hands and eat from them. Ieuan and Meidwen lived with their dad in a house in the heart of the forest. Their dad, Sannan, was the forester. He looked after all the trees and creatures of Coed Duon.

One evening the children were down by the River Rhymney, feeding the swans with left over vegetable scraps. An old lady appeared on the banks of the river. Her hair was long and white, her back slightly stooped with age. They knew her, had seen her before and knew that their dad was

always kind and respectful to her and had taught them to do the same.

'*Noswaith dda plant*,' said the old lady.

'Good evening,' answered the children.

She stopped to talk to them. 'I've made some cake, would you like some?'

'Yes please!' said the children and they followed the old lady to her little cottage. The cake was good and the children stayed and chatted for a while. Then they said they had better be going. Their dad would be worried where they were. The old lady didn't want them to go, so they stayed a bit longer. When it was getting dark outside and they knew their dad would be missing them, they tried to go again. 'We have to go home!' they said. But the old lady wouldn't let them go.

'Stay here!' she said and locked the door.

'Ieuan! Meidwen!' they heard their father calling them.

They shouted back, 'Dad! We're here!' but he couldn't hear them.

The old lady picked up a branch from behind the door. She struck the children, 'Swash, swish, you'd be better off as fish!' The branch was a magic wand from a hazel tree. The children began to shiver and to shake. They began to quiver and to quake. They were shrinking and turning to silver, with cold shining scales all over them. They were fish! Two silver, black-spotted salmon fish. The old lady picked them up, put them in her basket and hurried out the door.

The old lady went as fast as she could down to the River Rhymney. She passed Sannan on the way down.

'Have you seen the children? Have you seen my Meidwen and Ieuan?' he asked her.

'No,' she said, 'I haven't seen any children.' In the basket the children called out, 'Dad! We're here!' but he couldn't hear them. They were salmon now. They were the salmon children and they flipped and flapped in the old lady's basket.

When she got to the river, she threw them in, 'Splash! Splish! You'll be better

off as fish!' she cried. Splash! Splish! and they were in the water. Meidwen and Ieuan leapt and dived in the cold, clear waters of the Rhymney river. They turned and they tumbled with the river as it made its way down the valley and down to the sea. They found they could talk to one another with their minds. They were the salmon children. They tumbled and turned as the river threaded through Coed Duon. They leapt high and dived deep as the river came out of the forest and flowed past fields and farms. Down the River Rhymney ran, all the way down to the Severn Sea. Down the River Rhymney ran and down the Salmon children ran with it, all the way down to Môr Hafren.

Meidwen and Ieuan swam in Môr Hafren, the Severn Sea. When the winter winds roughened the waves they dived deeper and deeper to the land beneath. Deep down at the very bottom of the sea the salmon children found another country. They found the country of the Mer. They lived with the Mer people all through the winter. They learned all their stories and songs. They were the salmon children. They swam with the dolphins and played hide and seek with the shy seahorses. All through the winter they lived in the land at the bottom of the sea. They did not suffer through the winter storms, they were safe from the rain and snow. But all that time they never forgot their home in the forest and they never, ever stopped missing their dad.

One morning at the end of the winter they swam up to the surface of the sea. They could smell spring. They could smell home. 'Let's go home! Let's go and find Dad!' they said. Splish! Splash! The salmon children leapt and dived up the waters of the River Rhymney. They leapt high and dived deep as the river flowed up the valley past fields and farms. They tumbled and turned as the river threaded back through the forest, back through Coed Duon. They followed their heart's longing and found their way back, back to the rivers of home, back to the Blackwood. But how could they get back to their dad?

One moonlit night when they were close to home, they got caught in a fishing net. They were stuck in the net. They struggled and struggled but they couldn't struggle free. The fishing net belonged to one of the little people, the hidden people of the woods. When the little man saw the salmon children he knew that they were no ordinary fish. He knew that they were magic. He took them to show to the Primrose Queen, Briallen.

He took them behind the waterfall at Pwll-y-Bel to the court of Queen Briallen. Briallen looked at the salmon children and knew that they were magic. She knew that they were under a spell. Briallen called for a crystal vase to keep the salmon children in. She gazed at them as they gazed at her and Briallen began to sing:

*Fairy Flowers make a path,*
*Through the green woods to the heart,*
*Bring lost loved ones home again,*
*Bring lost loved ones home again.*

As Briallen sang, primroses sprang up in the woods. The primroses made a path along the banks of the River Rhymney. Briallen's song echoed through Coed Duon and the primrose path danced on. The primrose path danced all the way through the woods, all the way to Sannan's door, all the way home.

Sannan had never stopped searching for Ieuan and Meidwen. He had not smiled since the day his children had disappeared. His hair had grown white with sorrow. That morning in spring he opened his door to a primrose path. He heard Briallen's song and his heart began to lighten. He followed the path and his heart began to hope. Sannan followed the flower path down to the river, down to Pwll y Bêl Falls. On the riverbank he found Briallen waiting for him.

She was dressed all in green and wore a crown of primroses in her long, black hair. She led him behind the waterfall into the court, and into another world.

When the salmon children saw their dad they called to him, 'Dad we're here!' but he couldn't hear them. They were salmon. Meidwen and Ieuan leapt free from the crystal vase. They leapt high,

so high that they tumbled somersaults through the air. Briallen struck them with a branch, a magic wand from the hazel tree. As they fell through the air the children began to change. They shivered and they quivered. The silver scales that had covered them melted away. They reached the earth with their toes and feet. They were themselves again. They hugged and kissed one another and laughed and cried all at the same time. They thanked Briallen. When it was time for them to go home together they asked about the old lady. 'Leave her to me,' said Briallen.

Briallen walked through Coed Duon, her green serpent at her side. She found the old lady down by the river, weeping into the waters of the Rhymney river.

Sorrow had bent her back and turned her hair whiter than snow. Briallen looked at the old lady and knew that she was sorry for what she had done.

Briallen pointed the hazel wand and the old woman began to change. Her old bent back hardened, her feet became rooted to the earth and her toes dug down through the soil. Her skinny arms lengthened into branches and reached out over the water. Her long hair turned to leaves and covered her face. She became a tree. The old woman became a weeping willow tree. And her tears fell as leaves into the waters of the Rhymney river.

# 3

# The Lady
# of the Lake

Early one spring morning a young man was walking down by the lake in the Rhondda Fach. The lake was a green and silver mirror for the trees and sky. The small birds were singing in the oak trees on the steep mountain slopes above him. Yellow lillies were just opening their petals on the water. Everything made him happy. He looked down into the mirror lake and saw his own smile reflected there. The smile sent rippling circles all the way across the water to the other side. And on the other side he saw the lady.

He saw the young woman standing on the opposite bank. He waved and she waved back. He began to walk around the lake towards her. But before he could reach the place where she stood, she dived into the lake and disappeared under the water. He waited and he waited but she didn't come back up again. He looked around. There was nowhere she could have gone. There was no one he could ask. The small birds kept singing in the oak trees. He shook his head. He rubbed his eyes. Maybe he had imagined her.

When he got home after work that evening, his mother could see a difference in him. He seemed to be walking around in a dream. She asked him if anything had happened, so he told her. For a while she was silent and then she said, 'She's one of the Gwraggedd Annwn, the women of the lake. Best keep away.'

But her son said, 'Mam, I have to see her again. I have to talk to her.' He seemed so sad. She decided to help him.

His mother had learned all about the Gwraggedd Annwn from her grandparents. In the stories they had told her, the ladies of the lake could always be tempted

with freshly baked bread. Maybe they couldn't bake bread in their watery homes beneath the lake. The bread had to be just right though, not too hard and not too soft or the Gwraggedd Annwn wouldn't eat it. She promised to make him some.

The young man walked to the lake early the next morning carrying the warm baked bread in his hand. The lady was there, standing on the opposite bank. He waved the bread at her and she waved back. 'I'd like to talk to you!' he called. 'We could eat some bread together.'

He walked around to meet her. She stood and waited. They sat down together at the water's edge and shared the bread his mam had made. It was just right; it wasn't too soft and it wasn't too hard. It was perfect. They talked and talked and then they just sat by the magic mirror lake, listening to the small birds sing. And when they looked into the water they saw two smiling faces reflected there.

They met together every morning after that. They met throughout the spring and summer. By the time the autumn had turned the leaves to gold, they had fallen in love. They decided to get married. The lady of the lake promised to leave her underwater home and come and live with him on the farm at Rhondda Fechan. But she asked him to make her a promise. She asked him to promise that he would never disagree with her. She told him that if he argued with her, she would leave him and return to the lake. She would give him three chances. If he argued with her three times, that would be the end.

On the day she left the lake to come and live on this earth, the lake lady sang a beautiful song. The song made the water ripple and dance. Out of the water came white cows and black horses and a big brown bull. They were her wedding gifts to her husband and they were magic, just like she was:

*Dewch yma, Dewch yma,*
*Pedair Wen-Ladi,*
*Tair caseg ddu,*
*Bwla, bwla,*
*Dewch gyda fi,*
*Come along, Come along,*
*You four white ladies,*
*You three black mares,*
*Bull, Bull,*
*Come along with me.*

At first they were happy in the farm at Rhondda Fechan. But there came a day when they disagreed. They were at a funeral for an old man when the lady of the lake began to weep bitterly. She made such a fuss and wailed so loudly, not even the old man's children seemed as sad as she did. Her husband was embarrassed. That evening they argued for the first time.

'Why did you make such a fuss?' he said. 'Everyone was staring at you.'

'That old man hurt a lot of people in his life. I felt their pain and their sorrow. I know he will suffer in the next world because of the harm he caused. That is why I was crying. Now you have offended me once.'

When they had been married for a year, they had a child, a little boy. The boy was tiny. He was not strong enough to live long. Their baby son died after a few short weeks. The man was heartbroken. He had loved his tiny son so much. But the lady of the lake did not seem sad at all. She laughed and sang and went about the house with a smile. Her behaviour seemed so wrong; he could not understand it. They argued a second time.

'How can you be so happy when our son is dead?' he asked.

'Do you not think I loved him too? But my darling boy was not strong enough to live. He suffered. Now he is at peace. That is the second time you have offended me. Take care not to cross me a third time.'

One day the man gave one of their magic cows to a poor woman who lived in the house up the hill, at Tŷ Fry. When his wife found out she was furious.

'How dare you give away one of my cows without asking me first!' she said. 'It is good that you wanted to be kind to that poor woman, but you should have asked me. Those cows belong to me. That is the third time you have crossed me. Now I must leave you. I am going back to my home under the lake.'

As she walked home towards the lake, the lady began to sing. One by one her cows and horses and bulls came after her.

*Dewch yma, Dewch yma,*
*Dewch gyda fi,*
*Come along, Come along,*
*Come along with me.*

She dived into the lake and disappeared under the water. One by one the magic animals followed her. One by one they all disappeared under the waters of the lake.

The man from Rhondda Fechan stood by the water's edge and waited. He looked into the mirror lake and saw his own sad reflection there. His tears dropped into the water sending rippling circles all the way across the lake to the other side. But he never saw her again.

The lake is known as Llyn y Forwyn, the Maiden's Lake. If you go to Darren Park in Ferndale you will find it.

# 4

# The Giant
of Gilfach
Fargoed

Once upon a time, and a very long time ago it was, there were woods in the Rhymney Valley. The woods were full of oak trees and beech trees and hazel trees. And the woods were full of wolves and bears, deer and wild boar. And the woods were full of birds. The small birds sang all day and the owls called all night.

The woods were full of people too, people a bit like you and me, but little. The little people lived in the caves and in the trees and in the hollow banks of the Rhymney river. When the moon was full, the little people would dance and sing for joy in the woods. They loved the white, bright, silvery moon and were glad whenever they saw her.

One day a huge giant came to live at Gilfach Fargoed, the place at the edge of the woods. The giant was enormous! Wherever he walked the earth shook. In his massive hand he carried an iron staff.

Around the iron staff twisted a poisonous green snake. The poisonous green snake would twist and hiss and look for things to devour. When it saw its chance it would slither from the iron staff and kill whatever it could catch. It was a very greedy snake. The giant was greedy too. They didn't just eat when they were hungry. Together, the giant and the snake hunted down the creatures of the forest. The wicked giant ate whatever he could lay his hands on.

The giant built a huge stone tower in the middle of the woods. Now the little people hid. They stayed hidden in their caves and in the trees and in the hollow riverbanks. They didn't dare come out. It was too dangerous. They even hid when the moon was full. There was no more singing and no more dancing in the woods. The animals hid too and the small birds were too frightened to sing.

Deep in their hidden places, the little people wept and mourned the loss of their loved ones. The cruel giant had made their woods a dangerous place. They had to get rid of him. But how could they get rid of a giant? They were little and the giant was enormous.

Eventually, they came up with a plan. A few of the bravest of the little people crept out into the woods again. They whispered to the trees, the animals and the birds and asked them for their help. They asked the yew tree for some of her branches. With the branches from Grandmother Yew, the little people made a special bow and arrow. Then they asked the wise old owl for help. The old owl flew with the arrow and put it high in the branches of the apple tree, which grew on the doorstep of the giant's stone tower. Then they all waited for the full moon night. They all waited for the moon to shine silvery light over the woods.

On full moon night, they were ready. When the moon shone over the trees, the wolves howled, the bears roared, the deer and the wild boar bellowed. The giant woke up and he couldn't get back to sleep. He came out of his stone tower to see what all the noise was about. The wise old owl was waiting in the apple tree. She pulled back the bow with her beak and let the arrow fly.

Her aim was true! The arrow flew straight into the heart of the cruel giant and killed him stone dead. And when its master died the greedy green snake died too.

'Hoo, Hoo, the wicked giant is dead! Hoo, Hoo, the wicked giant is dead!' The owl spread her wings and flew over the woods, singing her song of joy. When they heard the owl's song, the little people came out of their hiding places to make sure it was true. It was! The body of the enormous giant lay stretched out cold. The little people were so happy, they began to dance and sing for joy. They danced around and around and around the body of the cruel giant. The birds sang too and even the animals joined in the celebration dance.

They danced all night and they danced all day and they danced the day after that. They danced for a week and then they had to stop. They were tired. There was also another reason for them to stop dancing. The smell! The giant's enormous body was beginning to stink.

So, the little people made a bonfire to get rid of the giant's body. The fire burned all night and it burned all day and it burned the day after that. The fire burned and burned and wouldn't go out. In the end the little people had to ask the Rhymney river to help. The river gave them some water to put out the fire.

When at last the flames were out, they found black, shiny stones in the place where the giant's body had been. The little people picked them up only to find more; they dug those up but there were even more of the shiny black stones underneath.

The little people realised that it was these shiny black stones that had kept the fire burning for so long. They called it coal. They dug as much as they needed and burned the coal to keep them warm and dry through the long winter nights.

Many, many years later more people came to live in the Rhymney Valley. They were big people. They were people like us. They chopped down the trees and dug deep, deep holes in the earth to get the coal out. The animals went. The wolves and the bears and the deer and the wild boar all left the valley. A few of the big people were greedy like the wicked giant and the poisonous snake. They didn't just take a little bit of coal, they wanted more and more. The more they had, the more they wanted. Many people got hurt or lost their lives digging for coal in the mines deep under the earth.

Now all the coalmines are gone and there are woods in the valley again. And in the woods the small birds sing all day and the owls call at night. But what happened to the little people? Do the little people still live in the woods? And do they still dance and sing for joy when the moon is full and white and silvery bright? I wonder.

# 5

# The Invisibility Seed

One midsummer's night Meg was walking home over the Garth Mountain. She was coming home from a party at her aunty's house. It was almost midnight, so Meg was walking as quickly as she could. It had been such a good party, she hadn't realised how late it was. Now she was hurrying home. She didn't want her mother and sister to be worried about her.

As she was walking through the ferns, Meg spotted a beautiful, red flower. She had never seen a flower like it, so she stopped to have a better look. Suddenly the flower burst open, just like a little candle flame. The little red flower shone so brightly that she could see all around, as if it were day. She stared. She had never seen anything like it. She walked towards it to pick it. She thought she would take it home and give to her mother. As she walked towards the flower, she heard someone laughing. She turned around. There was nobody there. She was all alone. There was no one on the mountain but her.

Meg walked towards the flower again. She heard the strange laughter a second time. Meg shook her head from side to side. She stretched out her hand towards the little red flower. It vanished. It was just as if its light had been blown out, like a candle. 'Oh well,' she thought, 'I'll just have to tell Mam about it. Not sure she'll believe me though. She'll probably think I've made it up.'

Meg carried on walking. What she didn't know was that some of the seeds from the little red flower had fallen into her coat pocket. The seeds were so tiny she couldn't feel them.

Meg carried on walking, but soon she was lost. That was strange. She had never been lost on the mountain before. Everything looked different. There were strange twisted hawthorn trees where the old oak was meant to be. There was marshy, wet ground where there never had been marshy ground before. The path led down, when it should have led up. It turned right, when it should have turned left. Meg walked through brambles and stingy nettles and fell into muddy ditches. She wandered and wandered for hours on the Garth, getting more and more tired, getting more and more lost.

By the time Meg managed to find her way home, it was almost morning. The sun was rising over the Garth. She was tired and muddy and wet and her legs were scratched to bits. She was so tired she couldn't even walk up the stairs to bed. She collapsed into the chair by the fire and fell fast asleep.

Meg woke up when her mother and sister came into the kitchen to make the breakfast. They walked past her, as if she wasn't there. Meg thought they must be angry with her for coming home so late.

'Oh, don't be like that,' she said, 'I didn't mean to be so late.'

Her mother and sister were silent for a moment. Then they both screamed at the tops of their voices.

'What's happened?' she asked. 'It's only me!'

They screamed again. Her sister ran outside to call the neighbours in to help. Her mother just stood there. She was fixed to the spot with her hands on the kettle. She was staring into space with her mouth wide open. She stared at the place where her daughter's voice was coming from.

Meg stood up. She had fallen asleep in her coat and she was still wearing it. Luckily for her, she decided to take it off at that moment. As soon as she took her coat off, her mother could see her.

By the time the neighbours came in, Meg and her mother were sat down

# The Invisibility Seed

together, having a cup of tea. Meg was in the middle of telling her about the little red flower in the fern and the strange laughter and how she'd got lost on the Garth. Of course, when the neighbours came in she had to start the whole story again from the beginning.

When he had heard the whole story, Meg's Uncle Jim said that he had heard about magic fern seed before.

'The fern only flowers on midsummer's night and the fern seed will make you walk invisible!' he told them. 'It will also lead you astray. That's why you got lost on the Garth.'

Meg's mother told her to throw the fern seeds on the fire. She didn't want her getting lost on the Garth again. So that's what Meg did. Or, that's what she said she did. But she did keep a few seeds hidden, just in case she ever needed to disappear again!

# 6

# The Sparrow Hawk

Once upon a time a young warrior rode through the gates of Cardiff. He rode on a willow-grey colt. He wore a cloak of the deepest purple, embroidered with golden apples.

One of the apples had been stained red with blood, his blood. The hilt of his sword was made of gold and his boots were of Spanish leather. He was one of King Arthur's men and his name was Geraint.

Geraint rode through the gates of Cardiff, following three strangers. He was following a little hooded man on an old skinny nag, a veiled lady in white on a white horse and an armed warrior on a warhorse. As he followed them through the streets of Cardiff, all the people came out of their houses to welcome the three travellers. They cheered to welcome the little man, the lady in white and the warrior. All the people cheered to see them. But no one cheered when they saw Geraint.

Cardiff was packed. Every house was full of men and armour and horses. Everywhere shields were being polished and swords burnished and armour cleaned and horses shod. Geraint asked a man what was going on, but all the man said was, 'It's the Sparrow Hawk!' He asked a woman what was going on, but all the woman said was, 'It's the Sparrow Hawk!' Whoever he asked the answer was always the same, 'It's the Sparrow Hawk!' Who was the Sparrow Hawk? Geraint followed the three riders until they came to the big castle in the centre of the town. He watched them ride in.

Geraint carried on riding. He was looking for a place to stay. He rode across the little wooden bridge over the River Taff until he came to an old tumbledown house. Sitting on the doorstep was a grey-haired man in worn-out clothes. The old man stared at Geraint for a long time and then he spoke.

'Young man, what are you thinking?' he asked.

'I'm thinking I've got nowhere to stay tonight,' said Geraint.

'Why don't you stay here?' said the old man. 'We'll look after you as best as we can. We haven't got much, but what we've got we'll share with you. My name is Ynwyl, Earl of the Mists.'

'Thank you for your kindness. My name is Geraint.'

Inside the house he met Enid, the old man's daughter. Enid's dress was all tattered and torn.

'Welcome,' said Enid. 'We haven't got much, but what we've got we'll share with you.'

Enid looked after his horse, gave it food and water and a comfortable stable to rest. Next, Enid went into town, and brought back supper. When supper was ready she called them to the table to eat. Geraint sat between the old man and the lady of the house and Enid served the meal. When they had eaten, old Earl Ynywl asked Geraint why he had come to Cardiff.

This is the story that Geraint told.

'This morning I was riding with Queen Gwenhwyfar near the Forest of Dean. As we reached the edge of the forest, we saw three strangers approach. We saw a little hooded man on an old skinny nag, a veiled lady in white riding a white horse and an armed warrior on a warhorse. We didn't recognise them, so Queen Gwenhwyfar sent her maid to find out who they were. The girl rode up to the little man and greeted him, but he ignored her. When she turned her horse towards the lady to speak to her, the little man screeched, 'You are not worthy to speak to them!' Then he lifted a whip and struck her face with it.

The poor girl rode back to us with her face covered in blood and tears. So, of course, I rode up to the little man and demanded an apology. He ignored me too. When I turned my horse towards the armed warrior, the little man screeched the same words again, 'You are not worthy to speak to them!' Then he struck me with his whip. The blood ran down from my eyes and stained the golden apples on my cloak. Of course, I was angry and I reached for my sword. But I reconsidered. If I attacked the little man, the warrior would attack me and without proper armour I didn't stand a chance. I wasn't ready to fight. So, I returned to the queen and asked her permission to follow the three strangers and avenge the insult. I followed them all the way here to Cardiff. I watched them ride into the castle in the centre of town. Do you know who they are?'

'I do not know the warrior's real name,' answered the old man, 'but they call him the Sparrow Hawk Warrior. He has come into town for the competition. Tomorrow a silver rod will be set up in the meadow and onto the silver rod will fly the sparrow hawk. The finest sparrow hawk you've ever seen. And the entire crowd of men and horses and weapons that you saw in town will come to the competition, and the best of all will win the sparrow hawk. And the warrior you saw has won the sparrow hawk for two years, and if he wins for a third he will be called the Sparrow Hawk Warrior from now on. If you wanted to enter the contest I could lend you my armour and my weapons, but you cannot fight unless you fight in the name of a woman.'

Then Geraint turned to Enid and asked, 'Will you help me get justice for Queen Gwenhwyfar? Will you let me fight in your name?'

'I would be glad to help you get justice for the queen. You can fight for the sparrow hawk in my name,' said Enid. 'And perhaps,' she added, 'you might be able to help our family too.'

Then Enid told Geraint this story.

'We have not always been poor. Once my father was the Earl of Cardiff and we were rich. We lived in the castle and we owned all the land down to the sea. But my father had a brother and his brother died. Just before he died, his brother asked my father to look after the lands until his son was old enough to inherit. My father said he would. Sadly, my father broke his promise to his brother. He was greedy and he kept all his brother's lands. He refused to give them to his own nephew, even when his nephew was old enough. His nephew made war on us and won. Now he is the Earl of Cardiff and he lives in the castle where we used to live and he owns all the land down to the sea. And we are poor and live here in this tumbledown old house. Perhaps if you win the sparrow hawk you could help us settle the argument. Will you help us get our old house and lands back?'

'I will do my best!' said Geraint.

By the time the sun rose the next morning, Geraint, Enid, her father and her mother were standing on the meadow bank. They heard a whistle, high and clear. Then they saw the sparrow hawk. Swift wings barred in brown and white, a flash of yellow eyes bright as the sun, the sparrow hawk flew! Everyone held their breath. The sparrow hawk soared high, high in the morning sky, then swooped down and down, cutting through the air like a knife, landing on the silver rod. The sparrow hawk perched motionless on the silver rod in the meadow.

The young Earl of Cardiff walked out onto the meadow and called, 'Who will fight for the sparrow hawk?'

The huge armed warrior, the man Geraint had followed from the Forest of Dean, gave a shout. 'I am the Sparrow Hawk Warrior! I will fight! I fight in the name of the Lady in White. If anyone denies her the gift of the sparrow hawk today, I will fight them.'

Then Geraint called out, 'I will fight for the sparrow hawk. I fight in the name of Enid, daughter of Earl Ynwyl.'

'Then let the Sparrow Hawk Contest begin!' announced the Earl of Cardiff.

The two men rode their horses to opposite ends of the meadow. Then they turned to face one another. Enid's father gave Geraint his lance and the little man gave a lance to the Sparrow Hawk Warrior. The signal was given. Each man spurred on his horse and the horses charged towards one another. The men held out their lances before them, gripped onto their shields and charged. Charge! The horses' hooves thundered over the meadow as the two men raced towards one another. Bang! Geraint's lance struck the other man, the saddle girths broke and the Sparrow Hawk Warrior was thrown to the ground.

Geraint jumped down from his horse and drew his sword. His attack was furious and fierce. The Sparrow Hawk Warrior fought back bravely. They pounded each other with swords until each one's armour was smashed and the sweat and the blood dripped down into their eyes. When the old man saw that Geraint was tiring, he called to him, 'Remember Queen Gwenhwyfar!'

Geraint summoned his last strength. He raised his sword and struck the other man. The Sparrow Hawk Warrior's helmet shattered and the warrior fell to his knees. He threw down his sword and begged for mercy.

Geraint granted him mercy. 'I will spare your life if you ride straight to Caerleon to ask Queen Gwenhwyfar for her forgiveness. But first you must tell me your name.'

'I will go now,' said the warrior. 'My name is Edern, son of Nudd. I am the brother of the king of the Underworld.' Then Edern rode away. Behind him rode the Lady in White and the little hooded man, and both of them were crying.

Then the young Earl of Cardiff called for Enid. She stood alone on the meadow. She raised her gloved arm high. There was a whistle and the sparrow hawk flew. Swift wings barred in brown and white, a flash of yellow eyes bright as the sun. Everyone held their breath. The sparrow hawk soared high in the sky and then swooped down and down, cutting through the air like a knife. The sparrow hawk landed still and quiet on Enid's gloved hand. The sparrow hawk was hers.

That night there was a feast in the tumbledown hall. Everyone sat down together. On one side of Geraint sat the young Earl of Cardiff and on the other side sat his old uncle, Earl Ynwyl. After they had eaten, they talked.

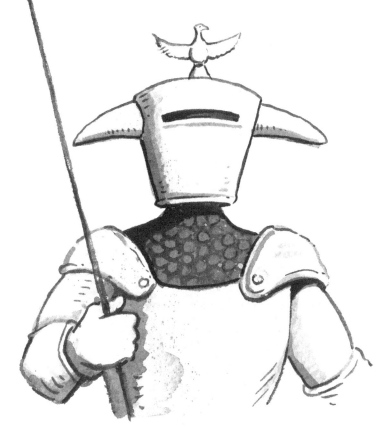

As Geraint listened to the uncle and his nephew, he realised that they both longed to be friends again. Geraint asked them if they could forget their quarrel. They said they could. They forgave each other. They shook hands and then they hugged.

So Enid's family were rich again and lived in the castle again and owned all the land down to the sea again. And all that

they had lost was returned to them, even down to the smallest jewel. All thanks to Geraint and Enid.

The next day Geraint asked Enid if she would travel with him to Caerleon so that Queen Gwenhwyfar could thank her for her help. Enid said yes. Enid rode out on a fine horse, the finest horse in the stables, but she wore her old tattered dress, because it reminded her of home. There were tears in her eyes when she said goodbye to her mother and father, but she was ready. The sparrow hawk flew high over their heads, as Geraint and Enid set out on their adventure.

This story comes from the Mabinogion. Thanks to Sioned Davies for her translation.

# 7

# Three White Roses

Once upon a time there was a shepherd boy called Tom. Tom looked after his father's sheep on Llantrisant Mountain. One midsummer's day Tom was up on the mountain and the midday sun was so hot it was burning him. It was too hot. Tom found a place to shelter from the burning sun. He found a cool, mossy rock in the heather.

As he was sitting there in the shade, he saw a girl all dressed in white. The girl had come from nowhere. One minute she wasn't there and the next minute she was. Tom sat very still. Hardly daring to breathe, he watched to see what the girl would do.

The girl in white began to hum a sad, strange song. As she hummed, she danced. She danced around and around, making a circle on the ground. In her hand was a bunch of white roses. As she danced and hummed, she scattered the white roses in a ring all around her. Tom watched. He was transfixed. He stared as she danced around and around. Then, suddenly, the girl in white vanished. Suddenly she wasn't there anymore. Maybe he had blinked.

Tom sat still for a long time. Eventually, he got up and went to look at the circle of white roses in the heather. The flowers were so beautiful he had to touch them. He picked up one of the soft flowers to take home with him, but when he looked down he saw that he had broken the circle. He didn't want to do that. He put the white rose back where it belonged. 'Sorry,' he said to the air. And then, all at once, she was there again. Maybe he had blinked. The girl in white was in front of him, standing in the ring of white roses.

She smiled at him and Tom knew that he had been right to put the flower back. She held three white roses in her hands. She reached out her hands towards him and gave him the flowers. Tom took the roses from her hands and said 'Thank you'. But the girl in white never said a word. Then she was gone.

Tom took the three white roses home and put them in a cup of water by his bed. In the morning he found three silver coins where the three white roses had been.

# 8

# Effie's Secret

It was there again, the dark shadow in the hedge at the bottom of the garden. Effie shivered. Her hands shook. She looked down hard at the earth, stared down hard at the spade and the weeds and the dirt beneath her fingernails. Keep working. If you don't look up, it won't be true. If you don't look up, he'll go away.

Every morning Effie was up in the dark to lay the fire and make the breakfasts. Then it was cleaning and scrubbing and washing and milking and feeding the 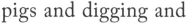 pigs and digging and weeding and no rest until bedtime. And at night she couldn't sleep. Effie was twelve years old, a servant at Prisk Farm, and something was

haunting her. She looked like a ghost herself, pale and thin, dark rings under her grey eyes.

One day the mistress called her into the living room to ask her what was wrong. She'd heard her crying in the night and thought she must be homesick. The mistress told her that she would be able to see her family in a few months' time and that now she was grown, it was her job to work hard and send money home. Effie shook her head. It wasn't that. She wasn't homesick. The mistress waited. Effie shivered and told her about the man in the shadows that no one else could see.

The old lady, the farmer's mother, sat in the chair by the fire and listened.

'There is no need to be afraid of spirits,' the old woman said. 'Just look at him and speak up and ask him in the name of God what he wants.'

Later that evening when Effie was clearing the table she saw him again. If you don't look it won't be true. She made herself look. It was true. Shadows blurred into the figure of a tall man dressed in black. Effie looked at him and the ghost looked back with his dark, hollow eyes. He looked so sad. Effie felt sorry for him. She spoke.

'What's wrong? In the name of God, why are you here?'

She heard a long sigh like the wind through dead leaves.

'Thank you, Effie. Thank you for seeing me and speaking to me. I have been waiting a long time. I was waiting before you were born. I am so tired, Effie. I need your help. Please help me.'

'Poor ghost, I will help you.'

'Follow me.'

She followed him down the steps into the cellar. He pointed to one of the old oak floorboards.

'Lift it up for me, Effie.'

She didn't think she'd be strong enough, but the heavy board lifted easily. Underneath, her fingers reached into the cold, damp earth and found a small box.

'Hold tight to the box, Effie.'

The ghost led her back up the stairs into the house, through the living room where the old woman sat by the fire. The old woman looked up as they passed and Effie knew she could see him too. Outside the yard was dark and still.

'Follow me,' said the ghost, and her feet left the ground. She was carried up into the air. Effie closed her eyes tight and felt herself floating, but held on to the box. The ghost was by her side. Effie opened her eyes and made herself look. She saw

# Effie's Secret

her whole world. She saw the farmhouse beneath her feet. It looked so small. The stars were all around her. She was floating through the darkness like swimming in the river. Effie looked down and saw the fields and woods and she saw home. She saw her own home where her mother and father and brothers and sisters were. She wanted to call out to them 'Look at me! Look, it's true. I'm in the sky with the stars and the moon.' She looked back down to earth and saw Hensol House far below. Then they were flying over the River Ely. The ghost spoke.

'Let go of the box, Effie. Let go now!'

She let the box fall from her fingers and the lid fell open. She gasped as she saw what was inside. In the starlight she watched it fall, then heard a splash far below as the box and the thing inside were carried down the Ely river and washed

away down to the sea. The ghost sighed and Effie felt peace.

Effie wanted to keep on looking and swimming through the stars but too soon her feet were touching the earth again and she was back in the farmyard, shivering. She heard the ghost whisper, 'Thank you Effie, thank you for helping me.'

Effie never saw the ghost again. When she was an old lady people would ask her to tell the story of what had happened that night and they'd ask her if it was true. She'd tell them the story and smile and then she'd tell them this, 'If you never look up, and you never speak out, you'll never know what's true and what isn't.' But when people asked her what was in the box, she'd never tell them. She kept that a secret as long as she lived.

# 9

# The Healing
# Snakes

Once upon a time there was a girl whose name was Ann. Ann lived with her family on a farm near the village of St Nicholas in the Vale of Glamorgan. When Ann was eight years old, she got ill. She had scurvy. The scurvy was horrible. It made Ann feel tired and weak. Her legs hurt when she walked and there were small, itchy red-blue spots on her skin.

Everyday Ann's father would carry her out into the garden to eat her dinner. Her parents had found that she ate more food if she sat in the garden, under the apple tree. Ann's gums and teeth were too sore for her to chew anything, so her mum gave her bread dipped in warm milk for her dinner. Everyday Ann sat under her favourite apple tree and waited for her friends to come. Yes, she shared her dinner with her friends, but her parents didn't know that.

Ann's friends would come slithering through the long grass to her side. They were snakes! Her friends were three snakes. Ann was always happy to see them. The three snakes would eat the bread from her hands and lap up the milk with their long snake tongues. While they ate, Ann would talk to her snake friends and tell them all her troubles. After dinner Ann would sleep under the apple tree and the snakes would lie beside her in the sun.

One day Ann's father was in the garden when the snakes came for their dinner. He watched in amazement as they ate the bread from her open hand and lapped up the milk with their long snake tongues. He was about to tell Ann off for wasting her food, when he noticed that one of the snakes had stopped eating and become very still. The snake seemed to be looking at Ann's hands. It seemed to be studying the red-blue spots. It looked at her feet. It looked at her face.

Ann's snake friend slithered off and returned a few minutes later with some green leaves in its mouth. It put the leaves on Ann's sore hands and feet. The other two snake friends slithered off too and came back not long after with more of the same leaves. Ann lay down under the apple tree and the snakes put the leaves on her arms and her legs and her face. Ann went to sleep and the snakes lay by her side.

Her father let her sleep. When he came to carry her back into the house the snakes slithered away. He asked her if she fed the snakes every day. Ann said she did. She thought her dad was going to tell her off for not eating all her food herself, but he didn't. Instead, he asked her if that was the first time the snakes had brought leaves and put them on her skin. She told him that they had done the same thing yesterday and the day before too, that this was the third time. She told him that the green leaves felt cool on her skin and that they stopped the spots from itching. After that day, Ann's father watched the snakes to see what they would do, but all they did was eat the bread from Ann's hand, lap up the milk with their long tongues and lie beside her in the sun.

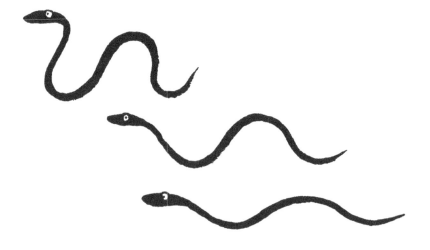

One morning, a few days later, Ann came running down the stairs. Yes, she was running! Her legs didn't hurt anymore! She ran out into the garden and back again, laughing. She gave her mother and her father a big hug. Her parents looked at her happy face and saw that it was clear. They looked at her hands and looked at her feet. All the red-blue spots had gone. The helpful snakes had healed her. Ann was well again! The doctor was amazed. Ann was completely cured, as if by magic.

Ann's father searched and searched for the leaves the snakes had brought, so that he could show them to the doctor, but he never found them.

Ann and her parents were always grateful to the helpful, healing snakes. And Ann never forgot to thank them. She never forgot to leave a bowl of bread and milk under the apple tree to say thank you to her three snake friends.

# 10

# Wild Swans
# at Barry Island

Once upon a time two men went to Barry Island. They went to Barry Island to shoot the wild birds. Barry Island was really an island in those days, so they crossed over to Whitmore Bay when the tide was out. They spent the long day walking the beach and shooting the wild birds out of the sky. When it was time for them to go home, the two friends found that the tide had come in and they were stuck on the island for the night. They decided to walk out onto the headland at Friar's Point while they waited for the tide to turn.

The two men watched the sun go down over the sea. As it set, the sun shone a golden path over the water. Two wild swans flew along the golden path of the sun. The swans flew side by side, their wings beating together in harmony. They were mysterious, beautiful and free. The men watched the swans land and glide gently over the waves to the shore. The swans stood together on the sand. They lifted their wings high and shook their feathers dry. As they did this, their swan feather cloaks fell to the floor and they weren't swans anymore. They were two women standing together on the sand, swan feather cloaks at their feet. The swan sisters stretched their long necks and lifted up their arms and yawned. Then they ran laughing into the sea, splashing one another in the waves.

The two men couldn't believe their eyes. 'Let's catch them,' they said. 'Let's make them our brides.' While the swan sisters splashed and played in the water, the two men crept down from the rocks and stole their swan feather cloaks. Then the men waited. At last, the swan women came out of the water and looked for their cloaks to put on.

'Are you looking for these?' one of the men asked.

'Give them back!' said one of the women. 'They don't belong to you!'

'You can have them back if you come and live with us, otherwise we're keeping them,' said his friend.

One swan woman began to cry but her sister wiped her tears away. 'Alright,' she said, 'we'll come with you,' and she took her sister's hand.

The two men stuffed the swan feather cloaks into the bags with the dead seabirds.

They gave their own overcoats for the sisters to put on. When the tide had turned, the swan sisters followed the men off the island.

The two men married the two swan sisters. The swan women learned to live on land. They learned to do all the ordinary, everyday things in this world. They learned to live in houses and to do the cooking and the cleaning and the shopping. The two men were pleased with their beautiful swan wives, so they kept their swan feather cloaks hidden. They didn't want their wives to fly away. The swan sisters searched and searched for their swan feather cloaks.

One day one of the swan sisters walked onto the road and into the path of a waggon. She walked right out into the road. The wagon driver didn't have time to stop and she fell under the wheels. People ran to her side to help her. She lay so still. Then she lifted up her head and stretched her long neck, reached out her arms and suddenly she was a swan again. The people all moved back. The swan sister spread her wings and flew. She flew! Mysterious, beautiful and free.

Her sister searched and searched for her swan feather cloak. Weeks turned to months and months turned to years and seven years passed. Seven years passed, but the swan sister never stopped searching for

her own swan feather cloak. And one day she found it. It was there, on the rubbish heap, covered in dust. Her husband had thrown it away. She stood in the yard clutching the dusty old cloak. She blew away the cobwebs and put the cloak around her shoulders. She stretched her long neck and spread her wings wide. The wild swan began to beat her wings, and then she flew. She flew! Mysterious, beautiful and free.

# 11

# The Lady of Ogmore Down

A long time ago a girl called Hawies lived at Ogmore Castle. Hawies' family were Normans. Hawies' great-great-grandfather was William de Londres, one of the twelve Norman knights who tried to conquer Wales. On her thirteenth birthday, Hawies' family organised a hunting party for her. She was awake very early that morning and, by the time the sun had risen, she was dressed and all ready to ride out into the woods with her family and friends and all the other fine Norman lords and ladies.

On her way out through the castle courtyard Hawies had to stop. She saw a young Welsh man tied up and held with chains of iron to the wall. She saw a fire burning and an iron rod heating up in its flames. Hawies felt sick. She knew what they were going to do. They were going to torture the young man. He must have been caught hunting in the woods. Welsh people were banned from hunting in the woods now and the punishment for breaking the law was torture or death.

'It's not fair!' she said to her stepfather, the Lord of Ogmore Castle. 'He was only hunting so he could feed his family. We should let him go!'

Her stepfather smiled, but his eyes were cold.

He was the Lord of Ogmore Castle, how dare she tell him what to do. But all the fine lords and ladies watched him and waited for him to speak. So the Lord of Ogmore Castle smiled a cold smile and gave orders for the prisoner to be released in honour of Hawies' birthday.

Her stepfather waited for her to say thank you. But Hawies had not finished yet. 'The local people need to hunt and to farm and to graze their animals in peace,' she said. 'We should let them have land of their own!'

Now she had gone too far. Her stepfather decided to teach her a lesson. 'Very well,' he said, 'if you want to be their champion, you can give them some land. They can have as much land as you can walk around from now until the end of the day.'

'Thank you,' said Hawies, and she got down from her horse and started to walk.

But her stepfather stopped her. 'Take off your shoes. You can walk barefoot.'

Some of the fine lords and ladies gasped and some of them laughed. Hawies' stepfather waited for her to stop, to take a few paces in her bare feet, to cry, and then to give up. But Hawies didn't stop. Hawies didn't give up. She took off her fine shoes and started walking in her bare feet.

Hawies climbed the hill, walking as fast as she could. The thorns and the brambles scratched the soles of her feet, but she kept on walking. The prickly yellow gorse tore at her fine clothes, but she kept on walking. Her stepfather's soldiers followed her, marking out the route she took. Hawies walked on in her bare feet, determined to walk as far as she could. She walked all morning. The sharp stones cut her feet until they bled, but she kept on walking. At midday when the sun was hot and high above her head, Hawies turned towards the sea, making a circle of the land. She walked all afternoon without stopping once to rest. Hawies walked all day. She reached Ogmore Castle just as the sun was setting. Exhausted and in pain, she sank to the ground. She had done it. She had circled the land and made a place for the people.

Now they would be able to hunt and to farm and to graze their animals in peace.

The land that Hawies walked is known as Ogmore Down. Ogmore Down has been free, common land since that time. The people say that you can still see patches of red ground. Those are the places where the earth was stained by the blood from Hawies' feet.

Lady Hawies was brave and kind. She lived a long life full of adventures. She is buried just down the road from Ogmore Castle, at Ewenny Priory Church. If you go there you can see the stone tomb where her body lies.

# 12

# The
# Sorrowful
# Witch

A traveller was staying in one of the villages along the Glamorganshire coast. One night he was woken by the sound of someone crying in the street outside his window. He had never heard a more sorrowful sound. It was the sound of someone groaning and moaning in pain and in anguish. It hurt the traveller's heart to hear it. He lay in bed and listened. There was silence. Then he heard the crying sound again, but fainter. At last he heard a sigh, a long drawn-out sigh, and then silence once more. The traveller got out of bed and opened the window.

He found himself staring into the piercing grey eyes of a witch. The witch's skin was chalky white and her yellow teeth hung from her jaw like tusks. Her hair was wild and red as fire. She lifted her two leathery arms and he saw that she had wings, like a bat. She flapped and flapped her wings and turned towards the sea. He saw a long black gown trailing, but could see that she had no body at all. As the witch flew over the sea, he heard her weep and then he heard the words, '*Fy ngwr, fy ngwr*, My husband, my husband'.

He watched her until she flew out of sight. The traveller stared out into the darkness for a long, long time before he eventually closed the window and went back to bed.

Maybe he slept. Maybe he didn't. Next morning his landlady told him there had been a terrible storm in the night. A ship had been wrecked on the shore. She said that many men had lost their lives and many women had lost their husbands. The traveller remembered the words the witch had cried, '*Fy ngwr, fy ngwr*, my husband, my husband' and he shivered. He told the landlady what he had seen and heard in the night.

'That was the Gwrach y Rhibyn,' the landlady told him. 'She is always seen and heard before a storm. She brings us a warning of sorrows to come. She is the Sorrowful Witch.'

# 13

# The Mystery of Kenfig Pool

If you stand by the waters of Kenfig Pool you might see the ducks swimming on the surface. But what do the ducks see when they dive deep? What do they see in the dark at the bottom of the pool? Do they dive all the way down to the old hall? Do they hunt little fish in the hall of the chieftain?

Once upon a time Kenfig was a town. It was a town full of people. At the heart of the town of Kenfig there was a magnificent round hall where the chieftain lived. The ruler of the town of Kenfig was a proud man, an arrogant man. He thought that he was the most powerful warrior of all.

One night the chieftain sat in his feasting hall and he heard a voice. He heard a voice on the wind though no one else was there. He put down his golden cup of mead to listen. The voice whispered in his ear, but there was no one to be seen.

The voice whispered, '*Dial a ddaw. Dial a ddaw*'. The chieftain shivered.

That night as he lay drifting off to sleep under soft, woollen blankets the chieftain heard the voice again. '*Dial a ddaw. Dial a ddaw*,' whispered the voice in his ear though he saw no one. Again and again he heard the words and the words that were whispered were always the same. '*Dial a ddaw. Dial a ddaw.*'

In the end he sent for his storyteller and asked what the words meant. So the storyteller told him this story.

'A long, long time ago one of your ancestors killed a man for no good reason. As that man lay dying, he put a curse on your family and your land. "*Dial a ddaw*" means his curse is on its way. His revenge is coming. It means that we need to leave this place now. It is too dangerous for us to stay here any longer.'

When he had heard the story the chieftain sat for a while in silence. Then he laughed, 'Ha! I'm not scared. Even if the old story is true, who could possibly hurt me? I am the most powerful warrior of all. I have the best fighting men at my command. This is my land. Why should I leave my own land?'

The ruler of Kenfig decided to hold a feast, to show that he wasn't scared. All the people of the town were invited to come. On the night of the party, the doors to the round hall were thrown open and the people poured in. What a feast it was! There were roasted meats, freshly baked loaves and cauldrons of steaming hot cawl. There were apple pies and blackberry pies and sweet honey cakes. There were dancers and singers, drummers and mummers, jugglers and fools. It was the best party anyone had seen for a long time. The only

person who wasn't there was the storyteller. When the chieftain called for stories, the storyteller was nowhere to be found.

At midnight they heard a voice roar like thunder. '*Dial a ddaw! Dial a ddaw!*' The candles suddenly all went out and the fire stopped burning in the hearth. The hall was plunged into darkness.

'*Dial a ddaw! Dial a ddaw!*' boomed the voice.

The ground began to shake and to quake. Then the water came in. Cold, cold water began to trickle into the hall. The trickle became a stream. The stream became a river. The water rose higher and higher.

The river became a lake. In no time at all the hall and the houses and the town of Kenfig all lay under the water. All that was left was a pool. Kenfig Pool.

Only one person lived to tell the tale. The storyteller shook his head and wiped the tears from his eyes as he stood by the waters of Kenfig Pool. If only the chieftain had listened to his story. If only he had not been so proud and so arrogant. The storyteller went on his way. As he walked he began to tell a story. He began to tell the story of Kenfig Pool.

# 14

# The Snake Lady of Swansea

The first thing he noticed about her was the green belt she wore around her waist. It was bright green and covered with strange spiral patterns. He asked her about it. 'Where did you get that belt?'

'My nan,' she smiled at him and her eyes were green too. Surprisingly green. He didn't know where to look. Lost for words, he smiled back.

He was a stranger in Swansea. He had come down from Anglesea for work. She was a local girl. She was kind to him and made him feel at home. He had never met anyone like her.

Before long they were married.

The night before the wedding she asked him to promise her something.

'If we get married, I will have to go away for a short time, twice a year. I'll go once in summer and once in winter. You must promise to let me go and never to ask me where I'm going or why.'

'When we are married you can come and go as you please and I will never interfere with your freedom,' he promised. They were married.

She left in summer when the blossom was on the hawthorn tree. He didn't want her to go but he remembered his promise. When she came home again he didn't ask her where she had been or why she had left. They were happy together.

She left in winter when the nights were long and dark and cold. He missed her but still he kept his promise. He was glad when she came home again.

In the second year he dreaded the coming of summer and was sad to see the blossom on the hawthorn tree. Why did she have to leave him? When she came home again he sulked for a while but still he said nothing.

But when she went away that winter, he was so lonely and the nights were so long and dark and cold without her, that when she came home he asked her where she'd been.

'You are my wife. We should have no secrets from one another,' he said.

'You made me a promise,' she answered, so he said no more.

The third summer came and he felt heartsick when he saw the buds appear on the hawthorn tree. He didn't understand why she had to leave him again. He wanted to stop her from going but he didn't know how. He went to see his mother to ask her what he should do. When his mother heard of her daughter-in-law's strange behaviour she wanted to find out more.

'She is your wife. She should have no secrets from you. Next time she leaves, follow her.'

He took his mother's advice. When the blossom was on the hawthorn tree and his wife left the house, he followed her. She took the path that led to the woods. He walked at a distance behind her, keeping to the shelter of the trees. In the green wood she stopped. She stopped and stood by the side of a deep, dark pool. She stood still by the water's edge for a long time. He watched, hidden in the trees, hardly daring to breathe.

At last, she spoke some words, too softly for him to hear, untied the green belt and threw it into the grass. Then she vanished. He stared. He rubbed his eyes; he shook his head. There was no sign of her. She had gone.

He stumbled out from behind the trees. He saw the green belt in the grass. It was swelling fat. It was spiralling around and around. It was moving, sliding, slipping. A green snake!

'Sssssssssssss.'

Frightened, he picked up a stick and threw it. The green snake hissed at him and vanished under the earth.

He waited and waited. When at last she came through the door, he pleaded with her.

'Why did you throw your belt into the grass in the wood?'

She went pale. 'You promised me. Why did you have to break your promise? Weren't we happy together?' The tears shone in her green eyes.

Now their happiness was gone. The man from Anglesea didn't know what to do to get their happiness back. When winter came he took her green belt from the bedside while she was sleeping. He lit the fire and waited until the flames were high. Then he threw the green belt into the burning fire. The green belt hissed and burned and crumbled to ash. When he went into the bedroom to check on his wife, she wasn't there. The Snake Lady of Swansea had gone.

# 15

# Elidyr in the
# Other World

Once upon a time there was a boy who ran away from school. The boy's name was Elidyr. He ran away from school because he was tired of being shouted at. He ran away when the teachers weren't looking. He ran as fast as he could. He ran down to the river. He found a muddy hollow in the riverbank and he hid. Elidyr never ever wanted to go back to school again.

Elidyr hid in the hollow of the riverbank for a long time. He stayed there until it got dark. When it was dark he started to miss his mum. He wanted to go home, but he knew if he did his mum would send him back to school again. Elidyr tried to sleep but the noises of the night kept him awake; the owl called and the fox called and there were strange rustlings in the leaves. At last he fell asleep, soothed by the song of the river.

Next morning the bright sun woke him. Now he was hungry. He nibbled on the grass like a rabbit, but he was still hungry. He wanted to see his mum more than ever. All day he stayed in the hollow of the riverbank drifting in and out of sleep, wondering what he could do and where he could go.

He must have drifted off again because he didn't hear the little men's footsteps. He opened his eyes to find them there. Two little men dressed in green with long, flowing hair and long, white beards. The little men smiled at him and told him not to be afraid. Their eyes twinkled and he wasn't.

'Come with us, human boy,' they said and their voices were ringing. 'Come with us to a happy place where you can play all day, a land without sorrow or anger.'

Elidyr liked the sound of that place, so he smiled at the little men and said yes. The little men walked to the back of the hollow, pulled back the riverweeds from the muddy bank and revealed a wooden door. They opened the door and went through. The tunnel in the earth was low and narrow so Elidyr got down on his hands and knees and crawled through after them. At first he was squashed, but the more he crawled the less squashed he became. After a while, he could kneel and lift his head. After a bit longer he could stand. He was shrinking! By the time the tunnel ended, he was smaller than the little men and they looked down on him.

The country they came to was green. There were trees and flowers everywhere. It was a bit shadowy, as though the clouds had covered the sun. The little men took him to a round marble palace in the woods where he was introduced to the king and queen. They wore crowns of gleaming yellow gold and his eyes were dazzled to look at them. The king and queen were kind. They asked him lots of questions about the land he came from. They shook their heads in dismay when they heard how unhappy he had been. They told him that theirs was a land without sorrow or anger. They often visited his world and didn't like the dishonesty and unkindness they found there.

The king and queen of the Other World invited Elidyr to stay. They said he could return to his world through the tunnel whenever he liked. He could go home and see his mum whenever he wanted to. So that's what Elidyr did, he stayed and played in the Other World and soon he had lots of new friends.

He went home to see his mother and told her everything. He told her how kind everyone was and he told her all about the gold and precious crystals. His mother wished she could see the wonderful country for herself. Elidyr decided he would bring her back a present.

He took a golden ball. He was playing with his friends in the fields, a game like bowls, but played with balls made of gold. He put one in his pocket when no one was looking. Then he began to make his way home. When he got to the dark tunnel, he realised that someone was following him. He was too frightened to look behind, so he kept on going. As usual he found himself gradually getting too big for the tunnel, first he ran, then he stooped, then he crawled on his hands and knees as fast as he could. There was definitely someone following close behind him now. When he got to the little door he pushed it open and ran as fast as he could over the fields and home.

He was out of breath when he reached his house. He tripped on the step and fell through the doorway. The golden ball fell out of his pocket and rolled over the stone floor. His mother saw it and gasped. The light of the gold filled the grey cottage like a sun shining. Then the little men came running in and picked up the ball. They looked at Elidyr with such a look of sorrow and disappointment. His face turned red with shame.

Elidyr

Elidyr ran after the little men to say sorry. By the time he reached the riverbank the little men had gone. He looked for the wooden door in the hollow, but it wasn't there. That night he cried himself to sleep. Next day he went down to the riverbank to search for the door. He searched and searched for the way back to the Other World but he couldn't find it. He never ever found it again.

His mother loved him and looked after him and after some time he felt better. One day he went back to school, he worked hard and did well. He grew up to be a teacher. He looked after people and helped them to be kind and gentle and honest, like the little people he had known in the Other World. He never forgot how happy he had been there. Even when he was an old, old man with white hair, tears would come to his eyes when he told this story and remembered the happy time he had spent in the Other World.

# 16

# The Treasure Cave

Once upon a time there was a man from Llanrhidian, on the Gower. One night this man had a dream. It was a dream about a treasure cave. The man's dream began in a dark, dark wood. He dreamed he was walking down a path through the dark, dark wood. The dream path led him to a rocky shore by the sea. He dreamed he found strange footprints in the sand and he dreamed he followed the footprints to a cave. Then the footprints stopped. They stopped in front of a deep, dark, gloomy cave.

At the back of the deep, dark, gloomy cave there was a door. An old wooden door with heavy iron hinges. Then he dreamt he heard music. The gentle music of a harp was playing in his dream. The harp played a lullaby. As the gentle music played, the iron hinges on the old wooden door began to creek. Slowly, slowly the door began to open. He glimpsed treasure shining on the other side of the door. When the door was open wide he saw gold and silver and precious stones. He began to walk through the door towards the treasure. That's when he woke up.

The next morning, the man from Llanrhidian remembered his dream. It had been so clear. He remembered everything that had happened in it. He even remembered the tune the harp had played. He couldn't stop thinking about his dream. He couldn't stop thinking about the treasure cave. Could the dream be true? He began to search through the dark woods, looking for a path that led down to a rocky shore. The more he searched, the more sure he felt that the dream was true. The more he searched the more determined he was to find the treasure cave. The man wandered all over

the Gower coast, searching and searching. He spent days and weeks and months searching. He never forgot the dream. Then one day he found it. One day he found the path.

He followed the path through the dark, dark woods, just like he had in the dream. He walked down the steep path to the rocky shore, just like he had in his dream. He found footprints in the sand, just like he had in the dream. He followed the footprints until he came to the cave. It was the deep, dark, gloomy cave of his dream. He stood in front of the deep, dark, gloomy cave and saw the old wooden door at the back. His hands shaking with excitement, he took a harp from his bag and began to play. He played the lullaby he had heard in his dream. Slowly the heavy iron hinges began to creak and the old wooden door began to open. He glimpsed the treasure through the open door. He stopped playing for a moment to gaze at the gold and silver and precious stones shining in the dark. The door stopped opening.

He played again and the heavy iron hinges creaked once more. When the door was open wide he walked right into the treasure cave.

The man put down his harp and began to fill his bag with gold. There was silence in the cave. Then slowly but surely, the iron hinges began to creak. The man was busy filling his bag with silver. He didn't know that the door was slowly closing. Too late, the door clanged shut. The man was trapped inside.

Somewhere along the Gower coast there is a treasure cave. You might follow a path through a dark wood one day and come to a rocky shore. You might see footprints leading to the cave but you won't see footprints coming out again. And if the sea is calm and the air is still you might hear the music of a harp playing an old lullaby.

# 17

# The Ox of Eynonsford Farm

Once upon a time there was a farmer at Eynonsford, near Reynoldston on the Gower. One night, when the moon was full, the farmer was woken by strange music. There was music coming from his cowshed! The house was a longhouse, with a room for him at one end and a room for the cows at the other. The farmer sat up in bed and listened again. He hadn't imagined it. There was definitely music coming from the cowshed. It was strange and beautiful music and he had never heard music like it before. It was a bit like bees buzzing and a bit like birds chirping, but there was a lovely tune in it. It made him want to tap his foot and dance, but it made him shiver a bit too. He got out of bed to find out who, or what, was down in the cowshed.

The farmer walked down the dark passageway, trying not to make a sound.

When he got to the animal stalls he peered in through the cracks in the door. There he saw little people dressed all in red, skipping and dancing on the back of his ox. The stall was full of little people! They were dancing on the ground, around and around, twirling and whirling like scarlet leaves on a windy day. The old ox seemed quite happy and stood patiently chewing while the little people danced on his broad back. And the little people were happy too. They were singing like buzzing bees and chirping birds and like themselves too. The man watched through the cracks in the door. He looked again at the old ox and saw that he was chewing flowers, not hay, and he'd never seen those flowers before.

Suddenly the ox stopped chewing and the little people jumped down from his back. The ox lay down, closed his eyes and fell asleep. Now the little people were climbing over the old ox's body and cutting his skin from his flesh and his bones. The farmer watched horrified, but he didn't dare stop them. He knew you must never make the little people angry. Instead, he watched as they cut the skin from the bones and hung it on a hook in one big piece. There was a whirring and a blurring, and a chopping and a cutting while the little people worked. When they had finished, all that was left of the poor old ox was a pile of bones and the skin hanging on the hook in the stall.

The moonlight shone on the white ox bones as the little people pushed open the door. They danced outside, carrying the pieces of the ox meat with them. The farmer waited until they had all gone then crept into the stall to see the remains of his old friend. Through the open door he saw a fire burning on the heath. The little

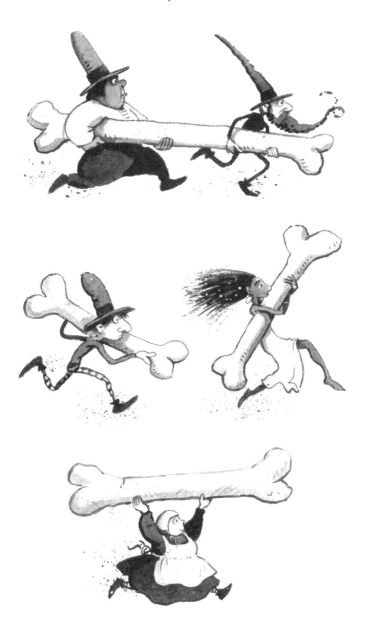

people were spinning around it. Around and around they went, diving and jiving like shining fireflies. He could smell the ox meat roasting. The little people were having a feast.

The farmer watched through the long night, unable to tear himself away. He stood and watched the little people dance around the fire in the full moonlight.

Just before dawn, they turned back towards the farmhouse. The farmer quickly closed the door and hid. He watched through the cracks in the wood as the little people danced in. They started to gather the bones. They laid them out carefully, making the skeleton of the ox. First the leg bones, then the back bones, then the neck bones, last of all, the skull on top. They kept on singing as they worked. When the skeleton looked complete, the song changed as the little people ran this way and that way. They seemed to be searching for something. Now their music was wilder, like the buzzing of angry bees. Eventually they stopped searching. As they began to sing a new song the farmer found he could understand the words:

*We thank you gentle beast,*
*For our delicious feast,*
*Time to wake now, dearest Friend,*
*Let skin and bone and body mend!*

The man watched through the crack in the door as the little people lifted the ox skin from the hook and placed it over the skeleton bones. The ox grew fat. He breathed out warm air and opened wide his deep, brown eyes. The farmer watched the little people dance out through the door, singing happily. When he could no longer hear their music he crept back into the stall. The ox looked at him with patient, deep brown eyes. He looked as well as ever.

The farmer told everyone this story, but no one ever believed a word of it. They thought he was making it up. They had to admit to one strange thing though. The poor old ox was missing one of his leg bones, though he managed just as well without it. The farmer said that was the proof. He said that when the little people put him back together again, they lost one of the bones in his leg. So his story must have been true.

# 18

# The
# Wishing Cap

One evening Molly Holly sat by the fire. She stared into the flames as she sipped her tea. Molly Holly was tired. She was tired after her long day's work. She had cooked and cleaned and washed and shopped and she hadn't stopped once. Not once had she stopped for a rest. Not until now. Now that the children were all fast asleep she had a moment to herself. At last. Molly Holly stared into the fire and wondered. What did Molly Holly wonder? She wondered why her children were always fighting and arguing and why they never helped her in the house. She wondered why her neighbours were always gossiping and why they never had a kind word to say about anyone. She wondered how she put up with them all and she wondered how she'd put up with them all again tomorrow. Molly Holly longed for a bit of peace. What she wanted was a nice rest. What Molly Holly wanted was a holiday.

Molly Holly got up and went out into the garden to throw away the tealeaves. There was the perfect crescent of a new moon in the sky. It looked just like a jewel. Seeing the new moon reminded Molly Holly of a story her gran used to tell her. A story about wishing caps. Gran had said that you could make a wishing cap out of a hazel branch when the moon was new. You had to make it quick, or it wouldn't work. A wishing cap!

Molly Holly hurried down to the old hazel tree at the bottom of the garden. She asked the hazel tree politely for its help, waited a moment, then twisted off one of the green branches. The soft and supple hazel branch made a circle under her hands. She looked up to the silver moon and put the wishing cap on her head.

'New Moon, New Moon, shining bright, Grant the wish I wish tonight!'

Molly Holly heard a swishing sound and she tingled all over like pins and needles. Everything went silver and green. She started to spin round and around. She closed her eyes to stop the giddiness. When Molly opened her eyes, she was on the seashore and the sun was shining. The little waves were lapping at her toes, so she took off her shoes and paddled. She

walked for a while, paddling in the warm water until she came to a house. The door was open, so she went inside. It was the sweetest little home for one, with a yellow door and whitewashed walls gleaming in the sun. Inside was a table all laid for breakfast with bread and strawberry jam and a pot of tea. There was a shelf full of books to read and a cosy armchair to sit in. In the corner of the room was a snug little bed, with warm woollen blankets and soft feather pillows. Molly Holly poured herself a cup of tea, took a book down from the shelf and settled into the cosy armchair to read.

But what happened at Molly Holly's house when her family woke up the next morning? They got a big shock when the fire wasn't made and the table wasn't laid for breakfast. They had to do it themselves. They had to do the cooking and cleaning and washing and shopping themselves. The children didn't have time to fight and to argue and their dad didn't have time to be bad tempered. They missed their mum, of course they did! When the neighbours realised that Molly Holly had gone, they all came in to help. They said how kind Molly had always been and how she would have done the same thing for them.

The days went by and the weeks went by and Molly Holly was still missing from home. One evening as the family sat round the fire staring into the flames, each one of them sad and lost in their own thoughts, each one of them missing Molly Holly and wishing she'd come home, they heard a knock at the door. It was two of the old aunties who lived down the lane. Their arms were full of hazel branches.

'There's a new moon tonight,' they said. 'We can make wishing caps.'

The children and their father followed the old aunties out into the garden. The aunties showed them what to do. The soft, supple hazel branches made circles under their hands. Then everyone put a wishing cap on their head and looked up to the new moon. It shone like a jewel in the sky.

'New Moon, New Moon shining bright, Grant the wish I wish tonight!'

They heard a swishing sound, then they all felt tingly, like pins and needles. Everything went silver and green and they began to spin. They span until they were giddy and then they all closed their eyes. When they opened their eyes, there was Molly Holly. She was standing in the garden as right as rain. Everyone hugged her and kissed her and cried tears of joy. The old aunties smiled.

Next morning the children made the fire and laid the table for breakfast and brought Molly Holly a nice cup of tea in bed. They were very pleased to see her, and so happy that she'd come home. The children promised to be good and not fight and her husband said thank you for coming back home. Molly Holly was really pleased to be home again too; she'd missed everyone and even been a bit lonely in her little house on the seashore. But from that day on, she always kept the wishing cap on a hook above the sink, just to remind everyone, just in case they ever forgot.

# 19

# King Arthur and the Sleeping Warriors

Once, a man from Glamorgan stood on London Bridge. He stood on London Bridge and watched the rest of the world rush by. It seemed to him that he was the only one standing still. His journey was over, for now. He had walked from Wales, all the way from Glamorgan. He had walked all the way from Glamorgan with the black cows, the sheep, the pigs and the geese. He had driven the animals along the ancient roads, over mountains and moorland, through valleys and woodland. Every night for three weeks he had slept next to them on the cold hard ground. He had watched over them through the nights and kept them safe. Now the animals had been delivered to the market at Smithfield and his job was done. Now he was on holiday. So he stood on London Bridge and watched the world go by.

As he was standing there, wondering what to do with his day, an old man came up to him. The old man had wispy white hair and a straggly beard. His coat was shabby and old with a faded pattern of moons and stars.

'Can I ask you where you are from?' the old man asked.

'None of your business!' he said in reply.

The old man ignored his rudeness and carried on. 'I can hear by your accent that you've come from Glamorgan. That's a very fine walking stick you've got. Is it hazel wood, by any chance?'

The man was proud of that stick. It was the best walking stick he had ever had. So he said, 'Yes, it is. I cut it from the hillside, from Craig y Ddinas, the hill near my home. It's lasted me all the way to London and has brought me luck on my journey.'

The old man smiled. 'It will bring you more luck yet. That stick comes from a magical hazel tree. Beneath the roots of that hazel tree is an underground cave. The cave is full of silver and gold. Take me there and you'll be rich!'

The man thought about being rich. He would never have to work again. He'd never have to walk to London again, or sleep with the animals on the cold, hard ground. Every day would be a holiday! He liked the thought of being rich.

'How do you know?' he asked the old man.

'Ahh,' answered the old man with a smile, 'I am a magician.'

The man thought for a moment and then he said 'Yes!' He agreed to take the old magician home with him to Glamorgan.

They set off next morning and walked the long way back to Wales. At night they stayed in inns along the way. The magician

paid for the food and lodging. At last they reached Pontneddfechan and home. He took the magician straight to the old hazel tree where he'd cut the stick. The old man said that he had seen the place in his dreams.

They got spades and began to dig. They dug out the roots of the magic hazel tree. Carefully they lifted it up and out of the earth. Then they dug some more until their spades hit something hard. They scraped back the mud to find a broad, flat stone.

When they had lifted up the stone, they saw steps leading down under the ground. They climbed down the steps and into the dark. The old magician led the way. They followed a narrow, stone-walled tunnel. After a while they came to a big, brass bell hanging from the roof. 'Don't touch the bell,' the old man whispered. They carried on in silence until they reached an enormous cave.

The cave was full of sleeping warriors. There were hundreds of them, all fast asleep. The warriors slept in a circle, with their heads on the outside. Every one of the warriors wore brightly polished armour. Their swords and their shields gleamed by their sides. They shone. But the brightest of all was the sleeping king. The king wore a golden torc around his neck. The scabbard by his side was encrusted with diamonds and pearls and embroidered in gold. In the centre of the circle, at the warriors' feet, was a pile of gold and a pile of silver. The light from the treasure and from the warriors' armour shone like the sun on a summer's day.

'Take as much treasure as you wish,' whispered the old magician softly, 'but only take from one of the piles.'

The man walked into the centre of the circle and filled his pockets with gold. The old magician took nothing for himself. When his pockets were bulging with shining gold coins they left the cave. They made their way back through the narrow, stone-walled tunnel. When he reached the big, brass bell, the gold in his pocket clinked and chinked against the metal. The bell began to ring.

There was a rustling sound form the cave behind them. One of the warriors was waking up. Then they heard a voice calling to them. It was a deep voice, a low voice. '*A ddaeth yr awr*? Is it day?' asked the warrior.

The magician called straight back, '*Cysgwch ymlaen*! Sleep on!' and the warrior was silent.

They waited. The warrior had gone back to sleep.

The two men made their way as quickly as they could through the dark tunnel. They climbed the steps and came up blinking into daylight. Carefully they put back the broad, flat stone and then heaved the magic hazel tree into place. They packed the earth around it. The old magician told the man he could ask three questions, three and only three.

'Who are the warriors?' he asked.

'It is Arthur, King Arthur who is sleeping here with his men. They will sleep until the time comes when we need their help again,' answered the old man. 'They are waiting for the time when the golden eagle will fight the black eagle. When that time comes the earth will tremble and shake so much that the bell will ring. When the bell rings they will wake. They will wake and fight until these islands of Britain are whole again and at peace again. That will be the last battle. After the last battle there will be peace forever more.'

'Why didn't you take any of the treasure for yourself?' he asked.

'Wisdom is better than silver and gold,' answered the wise old magician.

He asked his third and final question, 'Can I come back for more?'

'Yes you can,' the magician said. 'You have a lot of gold in your pocket now. You have enough gold to last you a long time. But, if you do need more, you can come back. But if you come back and accidently ring the bell you must remember the words to say. If the warriors wake and ask "*A ddaeth yr awr*? Is it day?", you must answer them "*Cysgwch ymlaen*! Sleep on!". Those are the only words that will send them back to sleep. Don't forget them, or it will be the worse for you.'

The man never saw the old magician again. For a long time he was rich and every day was a holiday. He bought the best of everything and treated all his family and friends to whatever they wished for.

But there came a day when the last gold coin had been spent. And he wanted more.

One day he went to the magic hazel tree on the hill. He took a spade. He carried a sack. He wanted lots of gold. He wanted a sack full of gold! He dug the roots of the old tree and heaved the hazel out of the ground. He dug and dug until he reached the broad, flat stone. Then he climbed down the steps, into the dark. It was so silent in the stone-walled tunnel under the hill. The only sounds he could hear were the sounds his feet made as he walked. When he came to the big, brass bell he was careful not to touch it. At last he reached the cave where the warriors slept.

The light shone from the polished armour of the warriors and the golden torc of the sleeping king, but the only light he cared about was the light that shone from the pile of gold. He began to fill the sack. The more he put in, the more he wanted. It was *his* treasure after all, wasn't that what the old man had said? He filled the sack until it was almost too heavy to lift off the ground. As he struggled under the weight, he thought of all the things he could buy with all that gold.

He dragged the bulging sack through the cave and heaved it onto his back. He staggered down the dark tunnel. He was panting and out of breath. When he reached the big, brass bell the sack full of gold clanged it and banged it. The bell rang out, loud and clear. The man stopped. His heart thudded in his chest. He heard a noise coming from the cave behind him.

The warriors were waking up. He heard their voices call to him as loud as thunder, '*A ddaeth yr awr?* Is it day?' they asked. And his mind went blank. His heart was beating so fast and their voices were so loud and he was shaking so much that he forgot the words the magician had taught him. He opened his mouth to speak, but nothing came out.

He heard the warriors' running footsteps coming down the corridor towards him. Then, everything went black.

When the man woke up he was all alone on the hillside. Someone had put back the stone and the earth and the magic hazel tree. The sack of gold was gone. When he tried to stand everything hurt. His whole body was bruised and aching. He struggled to walk back down the hillside. Eventually he made it back home.

When his wounds had healed and he was fully recovered he went back to Craig y Ddinas to dig under the magic hazel tree. He dug and he dug and he dug. But he never ever found again the cave where Arthur sleeps. And, so the old story goes, King Arthur and his warriors are still sleeping deep under the hill at Craig y Ddinas.

# 20

# Aunty Nan and the Skeleton Man

Aunty Nan was a storyteller. She lived in a little cottage in Melincourt village in the Neath Valley. Everyone loved listening to her stories. On winter nights they would gather round her fire and listen to her tales of giants and the little people, of ghosts and hidden treasure, of salmon children, swan sisters and snake ladies. Aunty Nan was round like an apple. Her hair was white as apple blossom, her face as wrinkled as an

old windfall, her eyes as black and bright as little apple pips. No one knew how old she was. She was very old.

One winter, people stopped going to Aunty Nan's house to listen to her stories. They still loved the stories, but they had seen a stranger go into her cottage in the evenings. He wore a long, grim cloak with a hood so you couldn't see his face. He rode a white horse that had cold blue eyes. Who was he? What did he want with Aunty Nan? They were scared of the stranger.

When Aunty Nan's nephew, Jack, came to visit, the people in the village warned him about the stranger. Jack said he'd sailed the seven seas and he wasn't scared of anything. He'd find out who the stranger was.

One dark December night, as Jack lay in bed, he heard a knock on the cottage door. There was no answer from Aunty Nan. There was a second knock on the door. Again there was no answer. On the third knock, he heard his aunty call out, 'Who is it?'

Then the answer came back, 'You know who'. Jack heard his aunty get up and unlock the door. Jack's bedroom was upstairs so he could look through the cracks in the wooden floorboards and watch what was happening in the room below.

Jack looked through the holes in the floor and saw a stranger in a long grey cloak come in and sit by the fire. The stranger's face was covered by a hood.

Aunty Nan smiled at the stranger. 'I expect you've come for another story. I'll make us a nice cup of tea and when we're sitting comfortably, I'll begin.'

Jack watched, as the two of them sat next to each other by the fire. The stranger listened carefully to Aunty Nan's story, though her voice was so soft Jack couldn't hear what she said. Every now and then the stranger would sigh or laugh or gasp with surprise. Jack could tell he was enjoying the story. The story went on for a long time. Jack could barely stay awake. It was very late at night, almost morning. Then there was silence. Aunty Nan sat back in her chair. 'That's all of them,' she said, 'all my stories are done.'

'Then we'll dance!' said the stranger. He stood up and threw off his cloak. Jack almost screamed, but stopped himself in time. The stranger was made of bones. He was a skeleton man. Jack's heart was thudding in his chest so loudly he thought they'd hear him. Maybe she did hear him, because at that moment Aunty Nan began to sing. She sang and held out her hands to the skeleton man. The two of them danced round and round the room. The skeleton man's bones clicked and banged to the

rhythm of Aunty Nan's song. The dance became wild as they whirled faster and faster. Jack was dizzy just watching them.

At last Aunty Nan sat down to catch her breath. Then she picked up her shawl and wrapped it round her shoulders. She looked around the little room and up once at Jack, straight at him. She smiled and her bright eyes twinkled as if to say, 'It's ok Jack. Don't you worry about me'. The stranger put on his cloak and pulled the hood over his bony skull head. Then, he opened the door wide.

Jack went to the window. The night was dark, but Jack could see enough. The skeleton man and Aunty Nan got up onto the back of the white horse. Cold, blue sparks flashed from the horse's eyes and silver sparks flashed from her hooves. There was a lightning streak. Then they were gone.

The pale winter sun was shining in through the window when Jack woke up the next day. He remembered what he had seen and heard the night before as if it were a strange dream. He went down the stairs. Aunty Nan was asleep in the chair by the fire. Jack gave her a kiss, but her cheek was cold. Aunty Nan's soul had passed away. All her stories had been told.

The destination for history
www.thehistorypress.co.uk

# Society for Storytelling

Since 1993, the Society for Storytelling has championed the art of oral storytelling and the benefits it can provide – such as improving memory more than rote learning, promoting healing by stimulating the release of neuropeptides, or simply great entertainment! Storytellers, enthusiasts and academics support and are supported by this registered charity to ensure the art is nurtured and developed throughout the UK.

Many activities of the Society are available to all, such as locating storytellers on the Society website, taking part in our annual National Storytelling Week at the start of every February, purchasing our quarterly magazine *Storylines*, or attending our Annual Gathering – a chance to revel in engaging performances, inspiring workshops, and the company of like-minded people.

You can also become a member of the Society to support the work we do. In return, you receive free access to *Storylines*, discounted tickets to the Annual Gathering and other storytelling events, the opportunity to join our mentorship scheme for new storytellers, and more. Among our great deals for members is a 30% discount off titles in the *Folk Tales* series from The History Press website.

For more information, including how to join, please visit

www.sfs.org.uk